CONTENTS

We Look and See

We Look and See

by WILLIAM S. GRAY, DOROTHY BARUCH,
and ELIZABETH RIDER MONTGOMERY

Illustrated by Eleanor Campbell

BASIC READERS: CURRICULUM FOUNDATION PROGRAM
The 1946-47 Edition

Scott, Foresman and Company

CHICAGO   ATLANTA   DALLAS   NEW YORK

Stories

Dick

Look, look.

Oh, oh, oh.

Look, look.
Oh, look.

Jane

See, see.

See Jane.

Oh, Jane.

Look, look, look.

Oh, oh, oh.

Oh, see.

Oh, see Jane.

Funny, funny Jane.

Baby

Look, Dick.

Look, Jane.

Look and see.

See Baby.

See, see.

Oh, oh, oh.

Oh, Dick.

Look and see.

See Baby.

Look, Jane, look.

See Baby.

Oh, oh, oh.

Funny, funny Baby.

Spot

Come, Dick.

Come and see.

Come, come.

Come and see.

Come and see Spot.

Look, Spot.

Oh, look.

Look and see.

Oh, see.

Run, Spot.

Run, run, run.

Oh, oh, oh.

Funny, funny Spot.

Puff

Jump, Puff.

Jump, jump, jump.

Run, Puff.

Run and jump.

Run, run, run.

Jump, jump, jump.

Oh, oh, oh.
Oh, Puff.
Look and see.
Oh, oh, oh.
Oh, see.

Tim

Jump up, Baby.

Jump up.

Up, up, up.

Jump up.

Come up, Tim.

Come up.

Up, up, up.

Come up.

Look, Dick, look.

See Baby and Tim.

Funny Baby.

Funny Tim.

Tim and Spot

Go up, Tim.

Go up.

Go up, up, up.

Go down, Tim.

Go down.

Go down, down, down.

Oh, Jane.

See Spot and Tim.

See Spot run.

Funny, funny Spot.

Funny, funny Tim.

Up and Down

Come, Puff.

Come and go up.

Go up, up, up.

Come down, down, down.

Go up and down.

Up and down.

Up and down.

Go up, up, up.

Come down, down, down.

Oh, Baby.

See Puff jump.

See Puff run.

Oh, oh, oh.

See Puff jump and run.

Puff and Dick

Come, Baby.

Run, run.

Run and see.

Look up, Baby.

Look up and see Puff.

Look up, Baby.

Look up and see Dick.

See Dick go up.

See Dick go up, up, up.

Oh, Jane.

See Dick come down.

See Puff come down.

Down, down, down.

Oh, oh, oh.

See Puff come down.

Look and See

Look, Spot.

Look, Puff.

Look and see.

See Baby and Tim.

Come, Spot, come.

Jump up.

See Puff jump.

Jump up, Spot.

Jump up and see.

Come, Dick, come.

Come and see.

See Spot and Puff.

See Baby and Tim.

Look, look.

Look and see.

See Baby Go

Look, Spot, look.

See Tim and Puff.

Jump, Spot, jump.

Jump up.

Jump up.

Oh, Jane.

Look and see.

See Baby go.

See Tim go.

See Spot and Puff go.

Oh, Dick.

Look, look.

Look and see.

See Spot jump.

See Puff jump.

Oh, oh, oh.

We Come and Go

We Come and Go

by WILLIAM S. GRAY, DOROTHY BARUCH,

and ELIZABETH RIDER MONTGOMERY

Illustrated by Miriam Story Hurford

BASIC READERS : CURRICULUM FOUNDATION SERIES

Scott, Foresman and Company

CHICAGO   ATLANTA   DALLAS   NEW YORK

Stories

Go, Go, Go

See, see.
See Mother go.

Go, Baby Sally.

Go, Sally, go.

See Dick go.
See Jane go.
Go, go, go.

Oh, Dick.

See Baby Sally.

See Baby Sally go.

Oh, oh, oh.

Go, Dick, go.

Oh, Mother.
See Dick and Jane.
Oh, oh, oh.

Tim and Baby Sally

Oh, Tim.

Mother sees something.

Dick sees something.

Jane sees something.

Look, look.

Baby sees something.

Tim sees something.

Oh, oh.

Baby wants something.

Tim wants something.

Oh, look, look.

Look, Mother.

Look, Dick and Jane.

See Tim.

Oh, oh, oh.

Puff and Spot

Baby Sally said, "Look, look.

Look and see.

See Spot and Puff.

Spot wants something.

Puff wants something."

Jane said, "Look, Mother.
Spot wants something.
Puff wants something."

Dick said, "Oh, oh.
Funny, funny Spot.
Funny, funny Puff."

Sally said, "Look, Mother.
Look, Dick and Jane.
Look and see.
Oh, see."

Come and Jump

Dick said, "Come, Father.
Come and jump."

Jane said, "Jump, Father.
Jump, Father, jump."

Sally said, "Come, Mother.
Come and see Father.
See Father jump and play.
Oh, oh.
Father is funny."

Jane said, "Oh, Father.
Mother can jump.
Mother can play."

"Oh, oh," said Baby Sally.
"Mother can jump and play.
Oh, oh.
Mother is funny."

Dick said, "Come, Puff.
Come, Spot.
Come and play."

Sally said, "Run, Puff.
Run, Spot.
Run, run, run.
Run and jump."

Dick said, "See Puff.

Puff can play.

Puff can run and jump."

Jane said, "Oh, oh.

Spot can not play.

Spot can not run.

Spot can not jump.

Spot is funny."

Come and See

Father said, "Come, Dick.
Come, Jane.
Come and see something."

Sally said, "Run, run.
Run and see it.
It is down, down, down."

Father said, "Look, Baby.

Up it comes.

Up, up, up.

See it work."

Baby Sally said, "Oh, oh.

See it work.

Work, work, work."

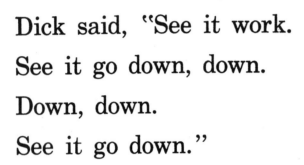

Dick said, "See it work.
See it go down, down.
Down, down.
See it go down."

Jane said, "Look, Baby.
See Tim go down.
Oh, oh, oh."

Spot and the Ball

Dick said, "Come, Jane.
Come and play.
Come and play ball."

Jane said, "Oh, Dick.
I can not find the ball.
Come, Dick, come.
Come and find the ball."

Dick said, "I see it.
I see the big ball."

Jane said, "Oh, Dick.
I want the little ball.
Find the little ball."

Dick said, "Look, Jane.
I can find the big ball.
Spot can find the little ball."

"Oh, oh," said Jane.
"See Spot run.
Spot wants the little ball.
Spot is funny."

Come and Help

Jane said, "Run, Dick.

Run to Mother.

Run and help Mother work."

Mother said, "Come, come.

Come to me.

Come and help me.

Come and help me work."

Baby Sally said, "Oh, Mother.
Sally is big.
Sally wants to work.
Sally wants to help."

Mother said, "Run, Sally.
Run to the car.
Run to the car and help me.
Big, big Sally can help me."

"Oh, oh," said Baby Sally.

"I see something in the car.

It is little Puff.

Puff wants to go.

Puff wants to go in the car.

Oh, oh.

Little Puff can go.

Little Puff can go in the car."

We Go Away

Dick said, "Spot wants to go.
Spot wants to go in the car."

Father said, "Down, Spot.
Run away, Spot.
You can not go.
You can not go in the car."

Jane said, "We can go.

Mother is here.

Father is here.

Dick is here.

Sally is here.

Away we go."

Dick said, "Spot is not here.

Puff is not here."

Jane said, "Puff is here.
Puff is here in the car."

Sally said, "Come, Puff.
Jump up to me.
You can go.
You can go in the car."

Dick said, "I see something.

Look down, Jane.

Look down and see something.

It is funny.

Can you see it?"

"Oh," said Jane.

"Here is Spot."

Jane said, "Come in, Spot.
Come in.
You can go.
You can go in the car."

"Away we go," said Sally.
"Away we go in the car.
Mother and Father.
Dick and Jane.
Spot and Puff.
Tim and Baby Sally."

Something for Spot

"Cookies," said Sally.
"I see three big cookies."

"Three big cookies," said Jane.
"Three big cookies for me."

"Cookies, cookies," said Dick.
"Three big cookies for me."

Sally said, "Three big cookies.

See the three big cookies.

One for Dick and one for Jane.

One for me and one for Spot."

Dick said, "Oh, Baby.

Where is the cookie for Spot?

Where, oh, where?

Where is the one for Spot?"

Sally said, "Here, Spot.
Here is a cookie for you."

"Oh, oh," said Jane.
"Where is a cookie for Baby?"

Mother said, "Here is one.
Here is a cookie for Baby.
A big, big cookie for Baby."

Sally Sees the Cars

Jane said, "Look, look.
I see a big yellow car.
See the yellow car go."

Sally said, "I see it.
I see the big yellow car.
The yellow car can go away.
The yellow car can go, go, go."

Dick said, "I see a blue car.
See the blue car go.
See the blue car go away."

Sally said, "Oh, Dick.
I want to go in the blue car.
I want to go away.
Away, away, away."

"I see a boat," said Sally.
"I see a big red boat.
I want to go in the red boat.
I want to go away in it."

Dick said, "See the boat go.
See the red boat go away.
You can not go away in it.
You can not go away."

Jane said, "Look up, Baby.

You can see something.

It is red and yellow.

It can go up, up, up.

It can go away."

Sally said, "I want to go.

I want to go in it.

I want to go up.

Up, up, away."

Dick said, "Come to me, Baby.
Here is something red and blue.
You can go up in it.
Jump in, jump in."

Sally said, "See me go up.
See me go down.
Up and down.
Up and down.
See me go."

Three Big Cookies

Jane said, "Come and play.

We can make something.

I can make cookies.

I can make three big cookies."

Sally said, "I can make cookies.

I want to make little cookies.

One, two little cookies."

"See my cookie," said Dick.
"Here is a funny cookie.
One big funny cookie."

Sally said, "See, see.
We can make cookies.
One funny cookie.
One, two little cookies.
One, two, three big cookies."

"Oh, look," said Sally.
"See Spot jump."

"Oh, oh," said Dick.
"Where is my funny cookie?
Where, oh, where?
Where is it?"

We Make Something

Dick said, "I can make a house.

A big house for two boats.

See my house.

The blue boat is in it.

The yellow boat is in it."

Jane said, "I can make a house.

A little house for three cars.

See my house."

Sally said, "I can make a house.

A big house for Tim.

Here is my house.

Tim is in it.

Tim can play in it.

Oh, oh.

Tim looks funny."

Jane said, "See Puff and Spot.
Puff and Spot want to play."

Dick said, "Look, look.
Down comes my big house."

Jane said, "Oh, look.
Down comes my little house."

Sally said, "Oh, oh, oh.
Down comes my house for Tim.
Down, down, down."

Spot Finds Something

Dick said, "Come here.
Come and help me.
I can not find the two boats.
I can not find my red ball.
Where is my little red ball?
Where is my yellow boat?
Where is the blue boat?
Where, oh, where?"

Jane said, "I can help you.

I can find two boats for you.

Here is one yellow boat.

Here is one blue boat."

Sally said, "I see three cars.

Here is my red car.

Here is my blue car.

Here is my yellow car.

One, two, three cars."

Dick said, "Oh, my.
See Spot work.
Spot can help me.
Spot can find something."

Sally said, "Look, look.
Spot can find Tim.
Oh, oh.
Spot is funny."

The Blue Boat

Dick said, "Oh, Father.

We want to go in a boat.

Here is a blue boat.

We want to go in it."

Sally said, "Go, go.

We want to go.

We want to go in a boat.

In the big blue boat."

Father said, "You can go.

You can go in the boat.

Jump in, jump in.

Jump in the big blue boat."

Sally said, "Here we go.

Here we go in the boat.

In the big blue boat."

Jane said, "I see two big boats.

A big red boat.

And a big yellow boat."

Sally said, "One, two.

I see two big boats.

A big red boat.

And a big yellow boat."

Dick said, "I see two little boats.

Two little blue boats."

"Oh, my," said Sally.
"Tim is not here.
Where is Tim?
Oh, Father.
Help me.
Help me find Tim."

Jane said, "Look, Sally.
See Spot jump in.
Spot can find Tim for you."

Dick said, "Oh, oh.
See Spot go."

Jane said, "See Spot.
Here comes Spot to the boat."

"Oh, Spot," said Baby Sally.
"You can find Tim.
You can help me."

BASIC READERS

THE NEW We Work and Play

THE NEW

THE NEW

We Work and Play

The 1956 Edition

William S. Gray, Marion Monroe,
A. Sterl Artley, May Hill Arbuthnot

Illustrated by Eleanor Campbell

SCOTT, FORESMAN AND COMPANY

Chicago, Atlanta, Dallas, Palo Alto, New York

Stories

Work

Work, Dick.

Work, work.

See, see.
See Dick work.

Oh, Dick.

See, see.

Oh, oh, oh.

See Sally Work

Work, work, work.

Sally can work.

See Sally work.

Oh, Dick.
Oh, Jane.
See, see.
Sally can work.

Oh, Sally.

Funny, funny Sally.

Oh, oh, oh.

Play

Oh, Father.

See funny Dick.

Dick can play.

Oh, Mother.

Oh, Father.

Jane can play.

Sally can play.

Oh, Father.

See Spot.

Funny, funny Spot.

Spot can play.

Look

Look, Jane.

Look, look.

Look and see.

See Father play.

See Dick play.

Look, Mother.

Look, Mother, look.

See Father.

See Father and Dick.

Oh, Mother.

See Spot.

Look, Mother, look.

Spot can help Dick.

Run and Help

Run, Jane.

Help Mother.

Run, Jane, run.

Help Mother work.

Come, Sally, come.

Come and help.

Come and help Mother.

Run, run, run.

Look, Sally, look.

See Spot work.

Funny, funny Spot.

Oh, oh, oh.

Spot can help Mother.

Puff

Look, Dick.

See Puff jump.

Oh, look.

Look and see.

See Puff jump and play.

Come, Jane, come.

Come and see Puff.

See Puff jump and run.

See funny little Puff.

Oh, oh, oh.
See little Puff run.
Oh, see Puff.
Funny little Puff.

Spot and Tim and Puff

Spot can jump.

Little Puff can jump.

Look, Tim, look.

See Spot and Puff play.

Look, Tim.

See Sally jump.

See Sally jump down.

Down, down, down.

Sally can jump and play.

Oh, Puff.

See funny little Tim.

See Tim jump down.

Down, down, down.

Tim can jump and play.

Big and Little

Come, come.

Come and see.

See Father and Mother.

Father is big.

Mother is little.

Look, Father.

Dick is big.

Sally is little.

Big, big Dick.

Little Baby Sally.

Oh, look, Jane.

Look, Dick, look.

Sally is big.

Tim is little.

Big, big Sally.

Little Baby Tim.

The Funny Baby

Come down, Dick.

Come and see.

See the big, big mother.

See the funny little baby.

Puff is my baby.

Puff is my funny little baby.

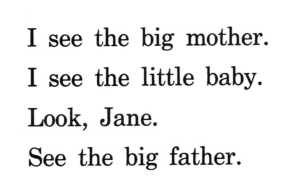

I see the big mother.

I see the little baby.

Look, Jane.

See the big father.

Look, Dick, look.

See something funny.

See my baby jump.

See my baby jump down.

See my baby run.

Oh, oh, oh.

Something Blue

Oh, Jane, I see something.

I see something blue.

Come, Jane, come.

Come and see Mother work.

Mother can make something.

Something blue.

Look, Mother, look.

I can work.

I can make something.

I can make something yellow.

Look, look.

See something yellow.

Oh, Jane, I can work.

I can make something blue.

I can make something yellow.

Oh, see my funny Tim.

Little Tim is yellow.

Baby Sally is blue.

The Little Car

Oh, oh, oh.

See my red car.

See my yellow car.

Come, Father, come.

Help Baby Sally.

Oh, Father.

I see my blue car.

I see my yellow car.

Look, Father, look.

Find my little red car.

Help Sally find the red car.

Look, Father.

I see the red car.

I can find the little red car.

See my cars.

Red and blue and yellow.

Red and blue and yellow cars.

Spot Helps Sally

Look, Spot, look.

Find Dick and Jane.

Go, Spot, go.

Help Sally find Dick.

Help Sally find Jane.

Go, Spot.

Go and find Dick.

Go and find Jane.

Run, Spot, run.

Run and find Dick.

Run and find Jane.

Oh, oh, oh.

Spot can find Dick.

Spot can find Jane.

Oh, oh.

Spot can help Sally.

Spot can play.

The Big Red Boat

Come, Baby Sally.

Come and see Father work.

See Father make boats.

Look, Sally.

The little boat is my boat.

I can make my boat blue.

See my little blue boat.

Look, Sally, look.

See my big boat.

I can make my boat red.

Look, Sally.

See my boat.

See my big red boat.

Oh, look, look.
See Puff jump.
See my boat go down.

Oh, look.
My boat is yellow.

The Boats Go

Oh, Dick.

The blue boat can go.

The yellow boat can go.

My little red car can go.

Look, look.

See my red car go.

Oh, oh.

See my red car.

See my red car go down.

Down, down, down.

Oh, Dick.

Help, help.

My little red car is down.

Up, up, up.

Up comes the little red car.

Look, Baby Sally.

See Dick help.

See the little red car come up.

Up, up, up.

The little red car is up.

Something Funny

Oh, Dick, look.

I can make Tim and Puff.

Tim is yellow.

Puff is red.

Make something, Dick.

Make something yellow.

Make something blue.

I can make something blue.

I can make blue cars.

I can make blue boats.

See my cars and boats.

See the funny blue boat.

See the funny blue car.

Look, Jane, look.

Up go the boats.

Up go the cars.

Up, up, go Tim and Puff.

Down come the boats.

Down come the cars.

Down comes Tim.

Down comes Puff.

Down,

      down,

            down.